AF427947

Coco June and Melanin: Poems from a Black Woman's Diaspora

Coco June
And Melanin:

Poems from a Black
Woman's Diaspora

Roe Braddy
Cover art and illustrations by Sami Hess,
Graphics by Ira Rebeca Covers

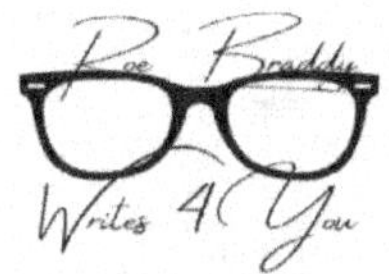

Coco June and Melanin: Poems from a Black Woman's Diaspora is a copulation of social justice poetry and short stories that give life to the Black woman's narrative. You will find yourself lifting your fist in solidarity when you explore the experiences of Black women who are living in marginalized communities, but not living marginalized lives. They are powerful, they have a voice, they are political, and they move in a way like no others do, these are the stories from and about Black women.

ROE,

THE POET

Like When

I need to grab hold of everything that
pushes me down and push back.

Like when you walk into a
room, and they turn their
heads wondering if your
melanin will make a stain on
their interior.

Like when mothers
have pressed their
oppressed beliefs
onto the pretty,
blond heads of
their baby girls,
when they only want to
dance, and wear pretty dresses,
and carry their colorless teddy
bears, and hold onto their barren
innocent minds.

Like when
you bring your wares to the
table of opportunity, and
you are told that your feet
don't reach the floor even
when you sit up straight—
so, you slouch.

Like when you see your
pennies falling, but not
from heaven becoming

smaller each day as they
become absorbed into a
politically twisted society
where old presidents
incite injustice on capital hills
that cause us all to
fall into distressed valleys.

Like when
kids sit in classrooms
forgetting that education
comes with no cost but
cost them the pain of using
dormant grey cells to keep
them out of jail cells.
Like when the cost-of-living
cost more than living
itself and the steps of the
poor are laden with
promises of good paying
jobs that take them to the
land of good living, but
only lead to the temple of
despair and foreclosure.

Like when we see the ending
of a good thing, like black
love, we cry a good cry and
hold our words in, never
voicing the pain of jealousy,
envy, and hate.

Like when we feel like we have failed,
never seeing that failure is nothing
more than getting off the boat at the
wrong dock, where we sit watching
both the tide and time roll away.

These things make me feel...

Like when?

Just an Old Chick Waiting on a New Revolution

I am just an old chick laying in the cut,
shaking my head—ego tripping.
This ageism is a real thing,
I am feeling it, right here, in the gut.

Martin had a dream, he talked about
mountain tops and freedom ringing.

Brown babies on the wall, just wanna get over
to the other side, some
of them are not fighting to get to
the top, they just okay with
their forty acres and a mule
that don't work.

Us old heads are sitting on the
edge of our seats waiting for
the new Martins, Malcolms,
and John Lewis power packers
to come our way.

There's a new generation of young
folks who see it their own way.

Let's not see through a glass
darkly and miss our
understanding of what
persistence for the disruption of
the old movement brought us.

Passing by, not standing for the
long haul, ears pressed to the
wall, hoping somebody got the
call, telling us that we are still in
our prime.

This time has not passed us by like
broken clock pieces that can't be
rewound.

New age, new wave, but there's still
nothing new under the old sun, that
beats the thoughts of freedom from
oppression into the heads of over
privileged, sassy mouthed babes.

I am just an old chick waiting on a new
revolution, hoping to still be around when
you proudly proclaim that you are now
beating the drum of freedom
and watching it reign.

I am just an old chick waiting on a new revolution.

Is It Eternal?

 Is it eternal? Will it remain settled
on my soul, ingrained in my spirit,
permeating my nostrils like
washed chitlings cooking on the
back burner of my momma's
stove, in the kitchen where my
sister's hair fried like breakfast
bacon.

 Is it eternal? Like my daddy's bad
back and busted knees, he got
serving in a war for a country that
thinks of him as a second- classed
citizen and only three-fifths of a man,
unlike "the man" standing in the
unemployment line beside him.

Is it eternal? Like catching
raindrops on your tongue
that soon turn into blood
droplets splattered across
urban sidewalks.

Like little white boys who tell you
it's okay if they don't do the work
now because they will grow into
middle class white men where all
things will come like golden gifts
on shiny silver platters.

Is it eternal?
Like heavy oppression that pushes black

folks down, making them forget about
those undreamed thoughts of success in
the white-washed marketplace.

Is it eternal, to be the token
one? The one with the
brownest face, the only one
that shines like a newly,
washed clean-to-the-bone
assimilated-chosen-
programmed robot.

Is it eternal to forget about
the ancestors who breathed
their last good breath crossing
the bloody banks of the
Jordan to reach the other side
only to discover that beans
don't burn on the grill and
good times are slow to come,
and there ain't no moving up
to the east side to no deluxe
apartment?

Does the heaviness of
carrying your melanin leave
you weak at the end of the day?

Does it give you cause to wonder why
the finger is being pointed at you? Do
you suffer from mistaken identity? Folks
telling you you'll never be, finding fault
with the space that you take up in the
universe.

Is it eternal?
Take no comfort in these temporary
afflictions, turn your face to the Son
because there is where eternity lies.

Push Thru

Mister, don't tell me to smile,
don't you see this emotional
labor that I am pushing thru
has not brought me any
offspring of comfort?

Push thru you say, push thru,
child, this black woman full
of weary burdens is looking
to the earth, the place
where I find the strength to endure.

Push thru you say, this black woman
waits on high for break thru. Push thru,
the afterbirth of humanity is stillborn,
it lies dormant in the earth's womb,
waiting for the day where it crowns in
equality, solidarity, and the expulsion of
racial disparity.

Break thru, push thru,
don't let us forget the
cords of injustice that has
been tied around our
necks.

Here in this place of pain is
where I have given birth to
the infant of hope, it is
swaddled tightly in a new day.

Push thru, pull
thru, rise, shine,
feel the joy of
your emotional
labor.

Smile.

These Crazy Things

You ask me these crazy things like I got
answers for all your unmet needs, these
things that cause me to lay awake at
night staring at the ceiling of my
unknown future.

I can't seem to find the need to follow
through, there's no solid ground under
this unstable force that holds me still and
causes me to wonder.

I wonder still of what the universe
offers to those who aimlessly wonder
through life, like they have lost their
ability to see life's efforts to attune
them to the place where strength
bends and endures.

I do wonder when they will see past my
darken skin and into the possibilities that lie
within.

I do wonder when life's hard places will become
soft, when what's heard on the streets will be
reconsidered vicious gossip and that people do not
dare bend their ears and lean into their own
understanding about whom they see when they
look at me.

I do wonder when peace will be still and the
thunder that steals the silence will heal my
hungry, hurting heart.

I do wonder about these crazy things.

Ode to Cairo

Little brown boy with twisted strands from
Cairo, braided into a prince's crown on your
head.

Egypt gave birth to you in full bloom,
pots of gold grow deep in your belly,
playgrounds and bishop's gardens rule
with bouncing balls and flashes of anger
that push your feet to full fuel.

They twisted wires around his neck and told
his momma he was a threat, Emmitt died and
never rose again, there was no Lazarus in his
bones.

The memory of his pain still causes us all to
strain just above the brim of injustice done to
little brown boys with wonderous eyes and
minds full of freedom dreams.

Don't walk up and put your hands on
someone's neck, the future that you hold is
held in loose hands, slippery as a slope it falls
quickly through your fingers, like stardust from
white shiny stars.

This moment will pass by it is a temporary
home for where your greatness will start.
Let your elders keep watch, as the saying goes, "You
are your ancestor's wildest dreams", let them dream
their dreams in and through you.

You walk a tightrope not balanced fairly; it does not sit on a line of equality.

This day will come and go, mark it down in your history books.

Little brown boy, play your games, live, love, and laugh for the future comes soon, little brown boy.

The Black Bridge

I am walking across the black foot
bridge. I feel like I've been through
this trodden earth before. My feet
are stepping in places where the
ancestor's shadows have laid.

My mind has wondered to the thinking of the
past. Drip drops of melanin fall from the veins
like blood droplets, tendons pulled from the
bone, heart stops, flutters, sweat pours down,
fear blossoms in bosoms that feed black and
white babies, some not free but held captive.

Some taken to the water and held
down, so breath came no more. I am
walking across the black foot bridge
where the air is thin, and life hangs
from a tender vine.

Black skin burned and hung from
trees that bare no sweet fruit, strange
whispers grow in the dark.

I am walking across the black
foot bridge where bodies once
fell dead. No more burdens to
carry, no more sins to hinder this
life.

Jordan's close, chariot swinging low,
ain't gonna worry no more.

I am walking across the black foot bridge.

Grandma Don't Play

Grandma came to school today. She didn't
come to dispense niceties; you see
grandma rules with a firm hand.

She doesn't take no second looks at what
don't seem right or misunderstood.

As the saying goes, "she don't play,
don't wanna play, and ain't even
thinking about
playing."

You best get your mind straight,
before she helps you meet your fate.

Grandma came to school today.

When I Wasn't Looking

My little boy slipped through my hands like rings
that are too big for my now thinner fingers into
manhood. Fingers that used to touch his baby face
that looked up to me in wonder.

He wondered about the world, his lips spawned
millions of questions, his eyes traveled over his
elders with anticipation of being a grown boy,
but he forgot it came with a black man's
struggles.

Finding his way, putting small, slender feet
into big man shoes, growing in spirts and
bountiful games with brown balls, sweaty
gyms, and coaching masters.

Long waits for degrees, promotions, and
gainful entry into his fullness came. There
were those reminders given in small daily
doses about life's constant talking, ticking
clocks that occasionally beat us into
submission of shortness.

Grab tight to the world's edges, hold onto it with
a master's grip. It's all so unstable at times,
sliding around and losing its security in realities
of yes, no's and maybes.

This is the disparity that money never buys too
much of, use it with hordes of wisdom and pounds
of good sense.

Don't waste droplets of blood, sweat and tears on
useless things that will cause your mirror of old
age to reflect regret.

Find your place, not amongst the stars, because they too
soon lose their illumination. Make way for blooming at the
axis of a spinning universe. This time is your time, grab it
by the edges and hold on.

I am on the Spectrum of Melanin

I am on the spectrum of melanin, like black
volcanic ash that falls on the litmus for brown
paper bag tests. I passed, but only in the
colder months, when the sun stops beating its
head on my red bone ancestry and causes my
melanin to leak from my skin like
unoxygenated blue blood from cold veins.

Sometimes drips of melanin fall out of
hidden places like stolen kissed droplets of
chocolate chips eaten away from the sinful
eyes of a hungry child.

The pain of what some say is too much
blackness haunts us, causing the shunning of
gifts, talents, and abilities to fall to the bottom
of the pot of pride, and high self-esteem in the
hearts of our tender young ones.

There are those of us who find our
greatness in the shades of amber and take
offense to the reminders of the Antebellum
fancy girl high-yellow.

Glowing shades of melanin
reigning from its original
source—the motherland of our
birth.

The spectrum of melanin is the cornucopia
of our truth—the source of our strength
as a people.

Wash off all that hinders you, take
your place amongst the flowers in our
garden and let your melanin bloom.

Trickling Dreams

Those trickling thoughts pour through your
mind and gather at the door of doubt, and
failure to find fortitude to believe in the
unseen, the what if's, the just becauses, and
the I am not sures.

Doubt is like a dripping faucet if you let it
continue, you'll have a flood of never
did's, and undreamed dreams that
manifest themselves to be left at the feet
of the would-be dreamer.

Don't let them put a stop to your
wondering moments, keep them at
the forefront of your to-do list. Don't
put off today for tomorrow, its
promise is not always kept.

Be diligent in your cause, keep your
shoulder to the plow, and your eyes
focused on the journey ahead.

Find your why and stop asking
when. Now's the time to let those
trickling thoughts—pour.

She Got No Rhythm

She's got no rhythm for the black man
who tells her, "I got you, Bae."

What she wished you had was two
pennies in your pocket that rubbed
together like good black magic and
fed this hungry child sucking at the
breast of disappointment, forgotten
promises and passed deadlines of
rent due please.

She got no rhythm for coming to
school and sitting on the playground
bench because they say her
youngest son is acting a fool and
that's just not cool.

But what they just don't know is there's
not enough of her to go around. She's
busy stretching a dollar and putting bread
and butter on the table to have paid
attention to when her life became so
unstable.

She got no rhythm for why all these
struggles have gotten her down. She's
lost her crown and the world forgot
she was a queen without a kingdom,
just unpaid bills, and not enough
meals to feed empty bellies of those
she gave birth to.

She's got fears that go way beyond
her years, she's cried plenty of tears
because she's left empty without
rhythm.

Good morning, Love

His hold on the world is not as elusive
as we think. There's a knowing that I
see. Those lines he wears gently
around his eyes tells me there were
days when the bitterness of life blew
the cold winds of despair, poverty,
homelessness, and hunger.

I can only imagine the younger version of
this stately soul, one where pride strut itself
down the street boldly and there was no
shame or sadness in the lines, he laid down
to all the sweet brown mommas that
crossed his path.

Another glance, a second thought and a
deep breath only holds those memories
loosely in his hands.

The strong breeze of hard times, lost
wages and love gone wrong blows them
freely from his grasp.

He sits on the end of the black bridge now, no
home, no way of showing his worth.

Black, old, homeless, some say a strain on society.
These words thrown on the wall like white paint—
pictures we don't fully see, sitting now, bent, but
not broken, holding onto a black trash bag, totting
his belongings and wares along the darken streets,
like broken pieces of black soul.

He smiles, his eyes twinkling like burnt, forgotten ambers that may have once reflected the light as father, brother, or son.

He smiles again, as our paths cross over the black foot bridge. He whispers these words— "Good morning, Love."

Spaces

Nails bitten back to the quick on
hands that nervously look for tiny
pieces of rest found in familiar
community spaces.

Spaces filled with voices telling babies
to hush, talking lowly of work done
for small time pay. Sitting amongst
books neatly stacked on store shelves
waiting for readers to come.

She stopped by with all her
belongings resting in grocery store
bags, speaking to unseen visitors,
thinking about meals she had and the
pillow where her head rested for
sweet dreams to come.

Now the sidewalk welcomes
her to its uncomforting spaces.
The un-homed ramble not
freely but paying the price that
no paycheck can cover.

I sit behind glass windows looking
out with full eyes at all that she
lost or never had to hold, wonder
resting at the back of my un-
swallowed tears.

The nails bitten down to the
quick on hands that find no
rest in community spaces.

My Words

My words lie on the end of my
tongue like bitter ash, like sweet
love juices that drip from their
unknown places and rest on my
curved spine causing me to sit
erect.

My words give birth and
memorize the sweet death of
terminal love struck, lovesick,
loveless dreams that have
expired from unnatural
causes like, no money, no
hope, and pain.

My words

rise

fall

sing

cry out

cry inward to untouched heavens, my words cry
the ugly cry in quiet rooms, and noisy filed spaces
where misogynistic, systematic, political thinking
twist themselves into the crevices where only my
words echo in my ears.

Calling the Griot

I want to die old and empty, empty,
like the elders who
told the stories of the
ancestral past.

Empty like the pockets of
those who picked cotton
and labored for the freedom
road.

I sit down at their feet and
listen to the stories that
spill from their lips like
pieces of gold falling from
treasured ships.

The Middle Passage—The
Motherland.
I want to grow old so I too
can be the Griot who won't
let the young forget what lies
below the past surface.

I want bones that ache from
memories of freedom marches
where victory was told.

I want eyes that have seen the
presence of the Lord.

I want to die empty and feel the presence of the elders calling my name.

Griot, Griot, come tell me stories.

No Money in Our Pockets

No money in our pockets, just
invisible treasures, and
bountiful hopes for the
brightness of our futures.

We were those clichés of
bright eyes and bushy
tailed, young, and
innocent.

We were the smell of fresh
squeezed lemonade poured in
glass jelly jars, hope, joy, and love
run abundantly.

First jobs in nursing
homes, old art classes,
grease paint washed off a
fresh face.

No money in our pockets, no bad
memories to haunt us of past
lives hoped to be forgotten.

Degrees, certificates of achievements,
bare walls waiting to be clothed with
their glory, still fresh faced, eyes full of
wonder.

No money in our pockets, but joy in
our souls, hope, faith growing past
the tips of our fingers, first love,

possessions now to hold, these we
lose quickly, but joy, hope and love
are eternal.

No money in our pockets, but hearts bursting full.
No money in our pockets.

Loc'd

It's a journey, you are still at the starting
line. The rat tail comb pulled the strands
of untamed, disrespectful fluff into a
threadlike crown of glory.

An inch longer it grew, pride set in a foot taller
was the walk. The Nubian queen was starting to
emerge.

No longer enslaved by societal standards of
political correctness, or Anglo-Saxton grade
of assimilation.

The journey began, loc'd.
He had a name, now only known as
40722. Leaving the last three digits
alone in their stance for a walk of
freedom they just called him "40", no
acre, no mule only fields of injustice to
plow through.

Mass incarceration, miles of
segregation, no hope, for restoration,
he just saw it as loc'd.

No lost causes here, we march through the
streets bolstering remnants of black pride. Our
faces numb, some wanting to commit suicide.
Only the weak left, no room for the strong.

She stood at the front of the line wearing her
Angela Davis crown, fist raised, heart open
ready to defend those young ones lost to the
street gangs and opioid slain.

He no longer put up a fight, there was no gun
that night, he should have walked away, no
pride lost was worth this cost of life vigor.
He's got jail time.

Babies pulling at her young breast, this whole
thing is one big mess. No job, no welfare line,
nowhere to go, so, she looks down at what
used to be her crown now a mass of tangled
hair, no fee for upkeep so she had to let them
go, now all she knows is what used to be, but
now what is loc'd.

Get up

Pushed down, running over, and laying
on the thrashing room floor, that's the
place where dreams go when they
don't know their worth.

Don't you listen to them who make
idol noises and sounds of jealously,
playing in the band and making you
feel like your drum ain't loud enough
to beat, like your strings ain't supposed
to be high strung and tight.

Go ahead chile, hold your head upright, don't
let them take away your fight.

Now's the time, it's supposed to be
done and done right, we ain't got no
time to be laying down, get up, get
up, and get it right.

Now's the time to find your fight.

Fight you say, put your fist down,
this ain't the boxing ring.

Use your head, it's all in them books
you read, it ain't found fighting out in
no streets.

Tomorrow ain't promised to the strong
nor the weak, it's the day that you're
looking at, this day, this time, for this
moment.

So, strike up the ambers of the fire
while they still burn high.

Don't lose the dreams on the
thrashing room floor.

A Kufi and a Cane

Walking, struttin' down the
street, proudly pushin' with
your cane tappin', tappin'
tappin'.

I see you moving and
using all your stride,
you tellin' the world
there ain't no reason
for you to hide.

Regal black man show us all
your pride. My mind pictures
who you are, but I clearly see
who you were back in the day.

You were something else, I can
tell, you were probably an alfa
male.

Giving the ladies a little
taste, not letting any of
your sweet juices go to
waste.

A kufi and a cane, walk
on by, all I can say is, oh
my, my, my.

A Lingering Thought

Lingering in the lining of my
cerebellum, soaking up cognitive
juices like the pot liquor of an
old ham bone boiling on the
back burner of the stove.

My mind is restless, it finds no
comfort in sleep, no delight in
simple tasks that keep it
occupied.

This invasion has caused me to
find no peace in sweet slumber,
this lingering thought fights me
like the devil finds vengeance on
Job's righteousness.

Mocking me, bringing me to
my emotional knees, there's
no peace I find that causes
me to store rest in my
restless moonlit moments.

These lingering thoughts cause my
nights to turn into preposterous
fighting cognitive wars that
threaten my sane side.

I rest the lid on the tip of the pot of my lingering
thoughts.

Lady Macbeth looked at her hands
and declared the blood to leave.

I look in the mirror and beg for peace
undone to move me to stillness sleep.

Pouring out my head, falling to the
floor, not letting them wrestle, but
finding a comforting spot, not too far
from the brewing pot.

Things That Twist my Spirit

There's a lot of things in the world that grab me
by the back of the neck and pull my eyes and
ears to full attention. There are times I sit back
in my chair wondering if the world has taken full
leave of its senses.

Jack be nimble, but sometimes Jack don't be quick.
Folks finding fault with the simplest things, leaving
each other with the bitter taste of hatred and bile
lingering along the edges of their lips.

Rodney said it best, he was surely under a little strain
when he uttered the words, "Can't we just all get
along?"

Kinda rhetorical, isn't it?

Momma used to say there is nothing new under the
old sun and the good Lord is the same today,
tomorrow and yesterday, well, some folks changing
stuff up in a drop of a hat.

I didn't think it was against the law to
eat Skittles but tell Trayvon that.

Our hands are up, and our mouths are open
wide sitting in front of our idiot boxes
praying and hoping we don't get shot.
Breonna, we see you.

We walk a fine line between love and
hate, riding down the street, feeling good
about our shiny brown faces, until our
necks are put under the strain. George,
we are here, feeling your pain.

My girl, Carlee finding invisible
children on the side of the highway.
What did you need that somebody
should have given you? Rest your
mind, dear. We are praying you find
your way.

Closing my eyes, I see the old
spirits of the past who used
to tell me that I would
understand the world and all
its bumps and grooves.
I am not sure I ever will.

I am watching the news, shaking my
head, holding my heart, clutching my
pearls, and calling on the name of
sweet Jesus.

These are the things that twist my
spirit.

The Sista was Stepping

I had a few minutes to spare, so I sat down and
let the cool breeze find my mellow spots. The
city's sidewalls cause a peculiar smile to ride
up on my face.

I laughed out loud at the little scooter boy who
wore his pocket-sized blue Crocs with pride.
He stopped short to show them off, full regale,
he did.

A man is never departed from his dog, best
friends they were, pulling each other along at
a steady pace. I felt a little fear curl up in my
belly as the muscular beast turned his head
my way, but with a pull of the leash, they
were back on the city beat giving me no time
of the day.

The Sista spoke words to herself, cussing
about some longtime friend that didn't
show up when she was supposed to. I tried
to pay her no mind, but there's something
to be said for being out of your right mind.

The breeze blew the city
walkers on by.

The Next Pretty Thing

Birth - day is coming. Birth and day
separated by each growing gray hair
that blooms from the short TWA I call a
crown, one more morning of stiff joints
and late nights.

Yesterday's call for young, and
beautiful has left me by the wayside,
instead it has been replaced with
time spent in the throes of life's
glorious storms and triumphant
moments.

These storms are what causes the full
moments of what growing older brings. I look
forward to sharing these graying aging times
with the young at heart.

Now, let's not get it twisted, ageism is
a thing, some folks think that a little
grey hair stops the flow of young
fresh thoughts.

I am still here, breathing, creating,
loving, and dropping a little wisdom to
the next pretty thing.

Backsplashes

I am standing in my kitchen with porcelain floors
and decorative backsplashes looking down at my
inherited collection of iron clad dreams, desires
and hopes.

As I look out the window and see azaleas
growing wild in the backyard where little
white boys with blue eyes and curly blond
hair run on weekly manicured lawns with
little black boys with almond eyes and
straight backs.

I think aloud wondering about the
contemplations my momma had on a cold
stove where hot dreams baked themselves
dry.

Its fiery red burners glazed pork'n beans and
fatback because times were lean, and life
was full of hard knocks.

The ancestors I know are clapping
loudly and praising the new day of
accomplished achievements and
stunning growth.

My momma's momma stood on the
dirt
floor looking down into the fire in the
kitchen of her nightmares praying to
avoid the back lashes of the master's
whip.

Picking up the cast of iron clad hopes and
sitting them on the blazing fire where the
desires to run for freedom for all its worth
left her belly yearning for the taste of sweet
black iron and earth.

I'm standing in the kitchen seeing dreams
running under the flowing facet of prayers
whispered in secret closets.

My eyes are closed, my dreams are spilling
over on porcelain floors, I am standing in
my momma's kitchen of hope.

Solitude

Sometimes one needs those moments of
solitude to let the tears come.

Sometimes stillness brings us closer to ourselves.

The words pour from somewhere in the
back of my spirit that contemplates
memories from the past.

Quieting the busyness of those who
rush by, finding hope amongst silent,
dark thoughts.

Moving quickly like souls that don't call
themselves ghosts; I find peace in my
solitude.

Finding Your People

When you lay eyes on your people the
feeling you get will find its way under
your skin, you know, it feels like warm
kisses from full lips, arms that grab you
up and hold you tight for all your worth.

When you find your people your soul cries out... I am
home.

When you find your people, your body can rest
itself in comfort like a feather bed for the mind.

Finding your people fills the empty
crevices and warms the spirit we all
have hope for.

Finding your people is like finding
home.

Book Dump

Don't worry about what you don't know,
worry causes wrinkles and who has time
for that?

Darrell Moore told us that there
were *No Ashes in the fire.*

The question remains and needs to be
asked, who keeps the fire burning?
Where are the talisman of the
universe that usher peace to our core?

James said, *Go Tell it on the Mountain,*
but Toni only wanted to live in The
Paradise of it all. *On and on,* right from
the bottom, Erykah said, *"the world
keeps turning peace and blessing
manifested with every lesson learned."*

I dream a world where the sun does shine
and *Caged Birds Sing* when they are
released from *The Temple of my Familiar.*

My Soul Looks Back and wonders *What
Would Happen if Beale Street Could Talk?*
Would we all be sitting quietly in *Giovanni's
Room?* waiting for our *Beloved?*

Tell me How Long the Train's Been Gone,
is it *Just Above my Head?*

Momma said, *Girl Get up and Wash Your
Face,* Stop *Falling Forward, This is Where it
Ends.*
I can't wait no more, *The Fire Shut up in my
Bones.*

I am resting in this quiet strength,
Living the Uncommon Life, praying for
Just Mercy before *Things Fall Apart*
and I get *Caught up in the Mix,* falling
for you.

I guess I'll see you Next Lifetime, *Does it All in With
Us?*
Go on now, *Sing you Home,* but *Stay with me,*
because
I am *The Woman in the Window, Gorilla my
Love,*
God Help the Child who has lost her way, I see with

The Bluest Eye and *I Wouldn't Take Nothin'
for My Journey Now, Sula, Sula,* I say, *Sula.*

Don't worry about what you don't
know.

Into the Day

Come fully into the day,
embrace the yearning to thrive,
flourish and see over the
horizon.

Come on in, leave your cares,
worries, tribulations, tire thoughts
and contradicting mindsets by the
front door of joy.

The joy that brings infection that
spreads across your face and
warms the corners of your lips.

Don't worry about the bags of
burdens you hold, let them go, drop
them by the wayside.

See them float into the sea of
forgetfulness, there is no hurry here,
no need to scurry around drowning in
a sea of busyness losing the source of
your strength and taking away your
gifts, talents, and ability to dazzle,
surprise, motivate and nourish.

Don't forget the dreams that flourish
in your eyes and bloom in your heart.
They are all worth the asking for.

Don't lose the thump in your beat,
the sound that pulsates in your ears
and rattles around in your head
causing cognitive juices to overflow in
abundancy.

I've come to remind you that the day Is young,
innocent, and pure. Pour your being into it, fill
it to the brim of overflowing possibilities—
they are ours for the taking.

Unraveled

You don't see the things that have started
to unravel like the hem of a poorly knitted
sweater. The sleeves have all come undone
leaving gaping holes of unrest and
emotional disturbances to my once
peaceful spaces.

The axis that once kept my
world spinning in your eyes
has come to a grinding stop.

These plates that I used
to juggle have fallen to
the floor leaving us both
empty right down to the
center core.

I am not sure that there is
anything left any more.

Mourning

It has left us tired, longing and
desiring for what used to be, we
hunger for the sweet breath that
used to blow over our faces like
sweet brown honey dripping from
the crevices of our mournful souls.

This pulse that beats
feverishly within my breast
knows no rest, its journey has
taken me to a place of no
return, mourning.

Shout hallelujah, the highest praise
for the lowest of us who sits at the
bottom of the tallest mountain
peak—mourning.

We collect no dust around our
feet, we lose no time, feel no
pain, see no troubles, hear no
cries because we have gathered
at the meeting place.

Mourning

Yesterday's grief echoes its
haunting laughter in our ear,
peace is not still, it moves
through the night taking life
from its sleeping victims.

Mourning

Crying has endured more
than just one night; we sit
on the edge of ourselves
waiting for joy to return
looking out of the glass
we see through darkly.

Mourning

Our arms have carried the burdens
we have not forgotten from the past
as we press our weary souls to the
crescent light, just above the
horizons where there is a place of
peace, this place holds us tight,
wipes our tears, comforts us amid
our deepest troubles—this place is
where we mourn no more.

Some Day Soon

Someday, one day soon,
its gonna come on in
like a monsoon, flying
and leaping, crawling,
and creeping.

It's gonna sit itself
down, make its way
around to folks it
ain't seen in a while.

Its gonna gussy up in
its own hi fa-looting
style, someday, one
day soon you gonna
see it come to pass
you best stay woke.
It won't be no joke.

Someday, one day
soon, ain't that what
they say, nobody
knows the time nor
the day.

Someday, one day soon,
it might be night, it
might be in the middle of
the afternoon.

There must be room
for it to soar and
take full flight.

Someday, one day soon,
we gonna look up and see
it right there next to the
moon, full of wonder with
its glory delight.

Fight it with all your strength,
and might, you'll know it's the
right time, you'll know someday,
one day soon.

Dismantling the Myth

Let me dismantle the myth,
there is room for you at the
top, don't let them tell you
there is not.

You won't have to do no side
stepping, there won't be a need to
squeeze by, slide in or hold up
your finger by hoping to be seen
invisible to those sitting high in
the seat of judgement.

Let me make it plain, and
beautiful in the eyes of the
beholder, there are no glass
ceilings that your blackness,
your strength, pride, and
ancestral lineage can't break
through, but you must
behold, and I do mean
tightly, on all that you are,
will ever set your steps out
to be.

Lay aside what others have
uttered in the echoes of their
small mindedness.

You are and will
forever walk in the
sunshine of your
gentleness, step aside,
let no shadows cast
doubt on seeing all
that your maker
has brought to fruition.

This my dear is not just a
hope, a dream, or a shot in
the dark for things yet to be,
so let me dismantle the
myth, there is room for you
at the top.

Now That We Are Here

When we came here the cotton was high in the field.
Our joy had not given us hope for freedom, we took
comfort in the knowing that God loved the child that
had its own.

We owned nothing, not even the scars on our bowed
backs, they too belonged to the master.
Audre told us "The master's tools will never
dismantle the master's house."

We still wait for the dismantling of generational
institutions that hold tight to pressing us down and
causing us to stumble into a disillusioned state of
social justice where our babies are still dying
senselessly on bloody sidewalks, where men in blue
forget oaths taken to protect and defend.

Before we came here, we ran through fields of
abundancy, we were kings and queens with authority
to rule over great nations.

We stood before men, naked and torn from
our land, now that we are here, we cry out for
freedom, we cry out for justice.

While we wait, we celebrate this day, the day when
chains fell from our bound arms, we raised our hands
to the sky and spoke with weight tongues of freedom
to come.

We are here, we will use the time to tell our young ones about the past. Tell them how we waited for freedom to come now that we are here.

A Pot on the Stove

It sits simmering slowly on the back burner of the mind. Leaving the seat of contentment to stir its contents brings the creator a blissful release of emotions. Creating can compare to nourishing our bodies with the food of the earth. Creation nourishes our minds and rekindles our tired spirits. The process requires a tender touch, a mind and a heart bent on patience and fortitude.

Get up now, put that pot of yours on the stove, let it slowly simmer until it is perfectly marinated into a rich, delicious concoction that mesmerizes every fiber of your being. Ebbing slowly from the tip of a brush, chipping the marble to recognizable form. Go on now, give us all your truth, be the wordsmith that delivers tantalizing prose.

The story slowly flows from the crevices of the cerebellum brewing, sauté it with a beat from a memory from a while back ago, not rushed to the end, but gently soothed into a collection of antiquated allegories specked across the pages like tears trickling down the face of a young lover who had lost their muse for life.

A brilliant mentor once told me a writer isn't a writer unless they write. Write we must, for words explode like rockets of raging verse, overflowing, and splattering from our fingertips. The artist takes paint to canvas, molding the depths of joyous, painful grandeurs of color. We sing a song of restless spirits that create works of passion, history, and triumphant moments.

Never cease your creation of what gives you restless nights and haunts the enter sanctums of your spirit, continue in your passions, go on now, put your pot on the stove.

Black Momma's Day

I am the mother to all the Black
babies in the world because I am
the sister to all the Black
mommas of the world.

We are all connected by the same birth pains
that gave us entry into the empty spaces of
our hurt feelings, broken promises by men
that seriously thought that the words doormat
were stamped across our foreheads in
permanent ink.

We walk down the same path. The one with the
hidden agendas, backward compliments coming
from mouths that have been whitewashed into
believing that reaching a handout to touch a Black
woman's hair is an acceptable microaggression that
we should simply be willing to bear.

We are sisters sojourning to places where our
degrees, intellectual abilities and words that spill
from our mouths that some say, "I thought you were
white, or "You are quite articulate for a Black
woman."

Sometimes we find ourselves telling all our truths,
spilling the tea while drinking the coffee to stay
woke.

The Motherland ain't in Africa no more, it's the
place where all Black mommas trying to keep their
Black babies off the streets and coroner's cold slabs.

This is just the beginning of this tale, because happy-
ever- afters are earned and not passed out like
lollypops laced with goodness and happiness.

See, we coming to you, not at you,
because we all Black mommas standing
on business.

Short Stories

Daddy-less Days

Sundays were special for this daddy's girl. You see, Sunday was the day when
Daddy would pick me up from Mommy's house and take me to church with him. Daddy and Mommy left each other when I was a baby. I guess they had emotionally stopped being a couple years before. I was the binding force that held together any assembly of unity between the two of them.

I do believe that my parents had become great theatrical performers. Their barely corrigible attitudes toward one another was evident, especially on Sundays. When daddy would come to Momma's house on Sundays her eyes would give her away every time; she held them somewhere between longing for what was in the past and hating what the present had become. I was just a young girl, but my inner voice, the spirit deep inside told me they both wanted things to be different. My Daddy's eyes had fire behind them, the flames were ablaze all for me. I think Momma wanted just a bit of the flame for herself; now that I am older, I've come to understand her angst.

She looked back at all she lost and hungered to have it back again. My grand momma always said that Sundays were the Lord's Day. I grew up wondering about the rest of the week, what claims did he have on those days? Those were the days without Daddy. I called them the "Daddy-less Days."

Those sorrowful weekdays lasted only for a while, but Sundays brought joy. I recalled the music; it warmed me like a blanket thrown over my shoulders on a frosty winter day. It was the Sunday music the choir joyously sang that would cause me to tap my foot in rhythm with the smiling faces of those around me. Daddy and I would sit in the back row of the church where there was room to stand. We would gently sway back and forth to the liquid joy that flowed from their lips.

Then there were the words that the pastor spoke, I watched others bob and nod their heads in agreement. Daddy's chest would rise and fall, his breath catching the words which seemed to bring peace to his uneasiness. Sundays were our best days, they seemed to only last for short spirts. I held onto them like rainbows after thunderstorms. Years have passed, those memories of my father are pressed firmly behind my eyes. When I close them tightly, I can see his gentle smiling face.

I bet a lifetime worth of pennies that Momma sees it too. The music played and we danced. It played in the background, but its rhythm beats a little slower now. Momma and I sit in the front row holding hands and patting our eyes dry. Daddy has gone to meet the God that he knew so well. Time won't come back again; those moments of my joyous Sundays are lost like ashes thrown to the wind. The music starts again, the songs cause fleeting pangs of both sorrow and joy to fill my hands with praise.

I lift them to the God that my father introduced me to those many years ago. The God that comforts me. No more Daddy-less days, because now my eternal one sits beside me holding my hand and dancing with me.

Gramgram

       I was 12 years old when my father was diagnosed with cancer. This diagnosis did not spring upon us abruptly, for years my father battled through a multiplicity of health ailments that he quietly dismissed. He was the only bread winner in our household. This daunting posture superimposed upon him seemed to give him a super-sized source of strength that neither my mother nor I could fully understand. My father simply did what needed to be done to keep our family of three afloat.

 The doctors said that he had maybe two good years left, if he was lucky. After receiving this diagnosis, he announced to the doctors that he was a man that did not believe in luck. He told them that he had spent a lifetime serving the Lord and that when the time came for him to part this world, he was going to do so on the terms that the Lord had laid down for him. There were no negotiations involving luck, only eternal promises of a home in heaven. With that proclamation, he ended all treatment and set out for what turned out to be the last three years of his life and the best three years of mine spending it with him until the end.

 I remember him telling my mother he was going to go out in style and take an early retirement before becoming too ill to enjoy his last days. During those times when my father felt well enough, we would get into his old Impala and drive over to Aunt Mary's house where we would spend a good portion of the day "sitting a spell" and talking.

I look back on those days of my father's quest to live his last years as a man who was full of life and not like one who was working on getting his affairs in order. Understanding now, what a gift he gave me; the gift of realizing that tomorrow is not promised. It may sound cliché, but because of his triumphant attitude about life, those lessons have stuck with me. I remember his passion for spending time with his family. He was all the way to the bone, "a family man."

Aunt Mary was my dad's favorite niece. She came to Pennsylvania when she was 23 years old, in hopes that living in the north would bring her a bit of the good life. She was part of the many black southerners who migrated north in hopes of escaping the oppression of southern Jim Crow laws. When she settled in Pittsburgh she went back to Santee, South Carolina and brought her great grandmother "Big Mary" to her new home back north. That was years ago. Daddy always said, "taking care of family was important."

Big Mary was not big at all. In fact, she was small in stature and probably weighted no more than a hundred pounds. Our family affectionately gave her that name because at 101 she was the oldest matriarch of the Whaley family.

She told us all the freedom stories about the last days after the Antebellum South. As a young girl I somehow understood that my father found the strength to take me to Aunt Mary's house because he knew it would be the place where our family's struggles and triumphs would be shared through the storytelling of Big Mary.

My father loved to sit with Aunt Mary at her kitchen table drinking black coffee and talking about their relatives that still lived in the south. Daddy always said that cancer didn't mean he was gonna give up on life and sit around and let us all watch him shrivel up and die.

My father and Aunt Mary would sit and talked while I was expected to sit in the living room with a big slice of cake and a glass of milk and keep Big Mary company.

Big Mary could always be found sitting in her Lazy Boy recliner covered with old quilts. She was always cold. I guess when you are 101, your blood runs real slow at least that's what Aunt Mary said. As I sat across from Big Mary, Aunt Mary would spread a napkin across my lap and hand me a slice of cake big enough for three people. That was fine with me because Aunt Mary's cakes were divine. She put down a wooden coaster where she placed a large glass of milk, served in an old jelly jar on the old mahogany coffee table that sat in front of me.

In her thick southern accent she'd say, "Girl, sit here with Big Mary and keep her company, and don't ya spill nothin' on that sofa, ya hear me?"

"Yes ma'am," I'd whisper back.

After Aunt Mary went back into the kitchen, I would wait a few minutes until Big Mary opened her eyes and sensed she was not alone in the room.

Big Mary didn't look like she was 101. She was a light-skinned woman with freckles and very few wrinkles. She had long white, thick wavy hair that Aunt Mary would brush out every day and style into two pigtails that were secured on top of her head with bobby pins. There was always a pair of wire rimmed glasses that sat low on the bridge of her nose.

Big Mary was completely blind, so she had no
practical use for glasses, I think she just liked
knowing they were there. When she opened her
eyes, they were cloudy, and the pupils were white.
Momma said she had an eye disease that made them
that color and that's why she couldn't see anymore.
   "Who that? That you girl?" she'd call out.
  "It's me Gramgram," I'd reply.

That was my special name for Big Mary. Gramgram
would close her eyes again and rest her head on the
back of her chair. This is when the storytelling would
commence. Gramgram would travel back to a time in
her childhood she remembered well. Her mother
had been born into slavery on a small plantation in
the south. I never knew where; I just knew that
Gramgram remembered the days of working in the
field alongside her mother and her two sisters as
sharecroppers.
        "Momma, no!" Gramgram would call out in a
half sleep.
 It was that moment when she would remember
when her mother had been badly cut by a machete
left lying in the field. She did not see the long rusty
blade until it had pierced the bottom of her barefoot.
Gramgram would recollect how she and her little
sisters had to use their petticoats to wrap up their
mother's foot and help her back to the little shack
they called home on the plantation.

"Jesus, make it stop bleeding, save our momma,"
Gramgram would say over and over. There were no
doctors that came to see about her, she just
wrapped her foot in whatever old, dirty bandages
she could find and continued to work in the field
until she died a week or so later from the spread of
gangrene.

After her mother's death, she and her two sisters
continued to work the field as young sharecroppers
with their father. There was no time for grief or
sorrow back then. At that time Gramgram, and her
two sisters stayed with their father until he became
old, and no longer able to work the fields. He was
buried on the plantation in an unmarked grave.
Gramgram and her sisters went their separate ways
a short time after that. She never heard from them
again. Gramgram's story made me feel sad. I would
sit still with my uneaten slice of cake on my lap as
Gramgram would call out. Tears would run down
from her closed eyes and her hands would be balled
up into tight fists.

"Give me some cake girl," she would softly moan as
she turned her head in my direction.

"Don't you give her no cake girl, she got the sugar, ya
know," Aunt Mary would bellow from the other
room.

"Yes ma'am, I won't," I'd say back. By this time
Gramgram would close her eyes and drift back to
sleep. Most of the time she would forget all about
wanting a piece of cake. Every day she would forget,
she only remembered the days of the past. I
wondered if I would grow up to be like Gramgram,
would I only remember right now?

Each visit was the same, Gramgram would tell a story from the past, ask for a piece of cake, and fall back to sleep while Aunt Mary would yell, "Don't give her no cake," and then we would pack up and go home. The slice of cake would be put in a piece of aluminum foil, I would take it home with me and save it for after dinner. Somethings never change, I can still remember all the visits to Aunt Mary's house, all the slices of cake that followed me home and all Big Mary's stories. These sweet memories were some of the last days I spent with my father. Big Mary and Aunt Mary are gone now, but their stories will always linger in my memory as special.

My Name is not George

It was my freshman year of college. My mother had told me if I was going to see my way through four years of school, I would need to find a part-time job. I had been raised to never fear hard work, so I found a job working as a nurse's aide in a local nursing home not too far from campus. I prided myself on being in touch with my roots. I was a young black college student who spent her free time reading Angela Davis' book, *Freedom is a Constant Struggle.* I wore big hoop earrings, an afro so huge that it touched the roof of a car when I got in and Birkenstock sandals. This look wasn't exactly conservative. for where I was about to work. I went to a smalltown state school where I was one of the minorities who didn't exactly blend into the woodwork of my environment's conservate views.

I plaited down my afro and traded my Birkenstocks for white Reebok high top sneakers and started my first day. I met with the head nurse, who was a stern woman who gave me a tour of the facility. She reminded me that my job was to adhere to the facilities policies for punctuality, dress code and service. I assured her that the policies would be on my priority list.
She gave me a look of doubtfulness but proceeded to introduce me to some of the residents.
Most of the individuals I met were pleasant and welcomed me as the newest staff member, however there was one exception. I can remember the day I encountered Gertrude Bartholomew. She was one of the oldest residents at the center. Gertrude was a stout woman who had bad knees and a disposition to match. One of my duties was to take the laundry cart down the hall and partner with another nurse's aide to put clean linen on each of the resident's beds.

Gertrude never took too kindly to me, whenever she saw me coming down the hall with my laundry cart, she would call out, "Get away from me you little nigger girl." I later found out that Gertrude was from the south and lived in the time where the laws of Jim Crow were the standard for all blacks. Each time I'd roll the cart down the hall and wait for her derogatory rant. It came like clockwork. At the end of my shift, I would go back to campus feeling defeated and a little less than. I needed the job, so I suppressed my desired to say anything back or to tell my supervisor about how I was feeling. It went on for weeks, there were times when I thought I could no longer bare it. Things changed for me when I met Mr. Thomas Whittaker.

Mr. Whittaker was in his eighties, and he happened to be the only black resident living at the center. I remember the day when we met. He was sitting outside of his room in a wheelchair waiting to have his sheets changed. Slowly lifting his head, he looked at me and uttered the words, "Is that you Baby Girl?" I looked around to see who he was speaking to, pointing to myself I asked, "Are you talking to me?"

"Yes, Baby Girl, I am talking to you. Now come on over and give your father a hug,"
he said in a deep, rich baritone voice.
I felt the tears well up in me as I hears the words "Baby Girl" coming from a complete stranger's lips. Those words were special to me because it was the endearing name that my father always called me. At the age of fifteen I had lost my father to cancer. My heart went out to this gentle spirit. Mr. Whittaker was in the beginning stages of Alzheimer's which

explained why he thought I was his daughter.

I remembered the haunting words of the head nurse when she reminded me that fraternizing with the residences during working hours was strictly prohibited. Looking around and taking notice that there were no senior staff members in the hall, I pulled my cart over and gave Mr. Whittaker the quickest hug. I could feel the heaviness lift from both our spirits. I needed the hug as much as he did. Stepping away and pushing my cart to the end of the hall I turned back to see the smile that appeared on Mr. Whittaker's face. From that day forward I would stop by Mr. Whittaker's room to talk. Alzheimer's is a horrible disease; it steals the present but somehow allows the person to hold onto the memories that occurred in the past. While it deteriorates the mind it leaves the person in a state of confusion and pain.

Mr. Whittaker had some days that were amazing, these were the days when he would recall memories of his younger self. He had been a Pullman Porter. After leaving the south, he took a job as a railroad pullman. He worked on the *Capitol Limited* train coming back and forth through Chicago, Illinois in the late 1940s. Working on the railroad was not an easy job. Mr. Whittaker had been subject to a great deal of racism and hatred. I had always been a history buff, when I discovered the history of George Pullman and how he had hired African American men to work for him and paid them little to nothing I realized Mr. Whittaker had been an intricate part of history. Despite all that he went through, somehow, he had remained a humble man.

At the end of my shift, I would stop by to tell him goodbye. I didn't work every day, so sometimes there would be a few days when we wouldn't see each other. I knew he remembered me when I would come back to work. He would wake up from a nap, look at me with a smile and say,

"Is that you, Baby Girl?" I would reply, "Yes, Mr. Whittaker, it's your Baby Girl." We did this for months. I knew the end of the semester was coming and I would soon be going home. This saddened me to know that I wouldn't see him over the summer. I didn't realize how close we had grown to one another until that day in the cafeteria.

Each evening dinner was served in the cafeteria at five-thirty. There were several residents who made it the social event of the evening. Gertrude Bartholomew was one of those residents. She would promptly push herself down the hallway and into the dining room claiming her seat at her regular spot. All the other residents knew that this was her "spot", no one dared to sit there. The only problem was, I was unaware of this tradition. My late afternoon class had been cancelled and my fellow nurse's aide asked if I could fill in for her at the dinner shift, so I had agreed.

Mr. Whittaker was one of the residents who enjoyed getting out of his room and going to the cafeteria for dinner. This evening seemed to be one of his best. As I pushed him down the hall toward the dining room we joked and laughed about some silly show that was on the television in the rec room. We were the first to arrive to the cafeteria. I pushed Mr. Whittaker to the first available table and then went to go and get his dinner tray.

When I returned, I was surprised by the bellowing voice of Gertrude Batholomew. As I turned to walk back toward the table, I heard her say, Why is this nigger sitting in my seat?" The entire dining hall grew quiet, and all eyes were on Gertrude. There it was again, that word. It echoed throughout the room like a sour note played on a piano or a fingernail being scratched across a blackboard. I sat the tray I was carrying down in front of Mr. Whittaker, when I suddenly realized it was not his, but Gertrude's. She continued to bite at me with her bitter words when she said, "I am not eating that after she's touched it."

I took a deep breath and stepped away from the table. What happened next staggered me even more. Slowly, Mr. Whittaker rose to his feet to the full length of his height. Stretching out his hand toward her he said, "Gertrude, I've simply had enough. I've spent half my life keeping my mouth shut afraid of white folks like you. Well, I am an old man now, ain't nothing left to lose. You ain't nothing but an old woman full of hate, you need to let go of it. I am tired of you. Jesus ain't gonna let your nastiness go untouched." Lowering himself back into his chair he took a deep breath and crossed his thin arms over his chest. Dinner went on silently for the next hour. Gertrude didn't stay. She quietly pushed herself back up the hall and requested that dinner be served in her room. After dinner, I pushed Mr. Whittaker back to his room and helped him into bed. Before leaving that night, I gave him a real hug, we both knew what it meant.

Several days passed before I worked at the center again. I remember coming back down the hall with my laundry cart and waiting to hear the voice of my good friend, "Is that you Baby Girl?" I never heard it again; Mr. Whittaker had passed away that same night after his confrontation with Gertrude. My father used to tell me never to hold onto the things that hurt you, it messes with your spirit. Mr. Whittaker let go of what messed with his spirt and when he did, he became free and unburdened. Rest in power, Mr. Whittaker.

Other Works by Roe Braddy

Scarred

Surrendered

Wading

A Seat on The Playground

The Red Box of Marbles (Children's Book)

The Royal Storyteller (Children's Book)

Our Voices (Poetry Anthology)

It's All Love (Romance Anthology)

A Good Church Going Woman (Kindle Vella)

Madam Knock's 2nd Street Beauty Parlor (Kindle Vella)

She can be reached at:
Roe@RoeBraddyProductions.com

Like her on Facebook at:
www.Facebook.com/RoeBraddy

Instagram

@roetheliterary

About the Author

Roe is a multi-genre author and a playwright. She comes from a long line of storytellers.
She is a retired educator who has always enjoyed poetry, short stories, and the theatre.
She has written and produced three stage productions and directed several for local theatres
and her church drama ministry. She is also the editor and chief of a local magazine.
 Roe has a love for vintage clothes and furniture and funky eyewear.
She lives in Pennsylvania with her husband and has two adult children.

9 798822 772251